Fergus the Sea Dog

For Rebecca and new baby granddaughter Molly

First published in Great Britain in 2004
by Piccadilly Press Ltd.,
5 Castle Road, London NW1 8PR

Text and illustration copyright © Tony Maddox, 2004

Cover design by Tony Maddox and Fielding Design
Text design by Tony Maddox and Louise Millar

Colour reproductions by Dot Gradations Ltd, UK
Printed and bound in Belgium by Proost

ISBN: 1 85340 729 1 (hardback)
1 85340 719 4 (paperback)

1 3 5 7 9 10 8 6 4 2

A catalogue record of this book is available from the British Library

Tony Maddox lives in Worcestershire.
He has written ten books for Piccadilly Press including the eight Fergus *titles and* Spike's Best Nest.

FERGUS THE FARMYARD DOG
ISBN: 1 85340 174 9 (p/b)

FERGUS'S BIG SPLASH
ISBN: 1 85340 388 1 (p/b)

FERGUS'S UPSIDE-DOWN DAY
ISBN: 1 85340 284 2 (p/b)

FERGUS AND MARIGOLD
ISBN: 1 85340 478 0 (p/b)

FERGUS GOES QUACKERS!
ISBN: 1 85340 566 3 (p/b)

FERGUS'S SCARY NIGHT
ISBN: 1 85340 631 7 (p/b)

FERGUS TO THE RESCUE
ISBN: 1 85340 771 2 (p/b)

Fergus the Sea Dog

Tony Maddox

Piccadilly Press • London

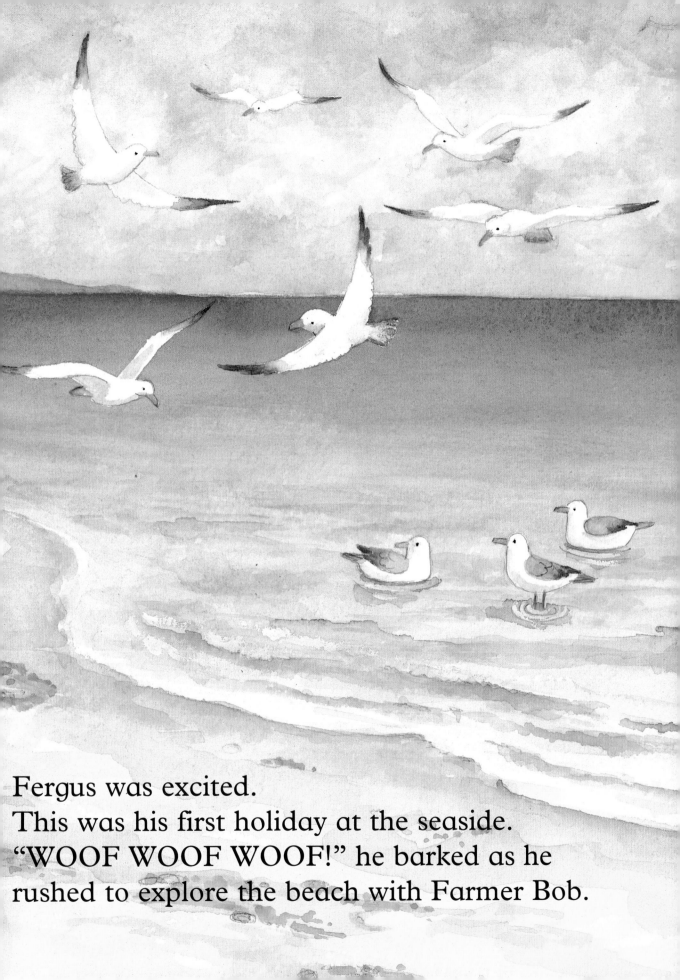

Fergus was excited.
This was his first holiday at the seaside.
"WOOF WOOF WOOF!" he barked as he
rushed to explore the beach with Farmer Bob.

There were so many things to do!

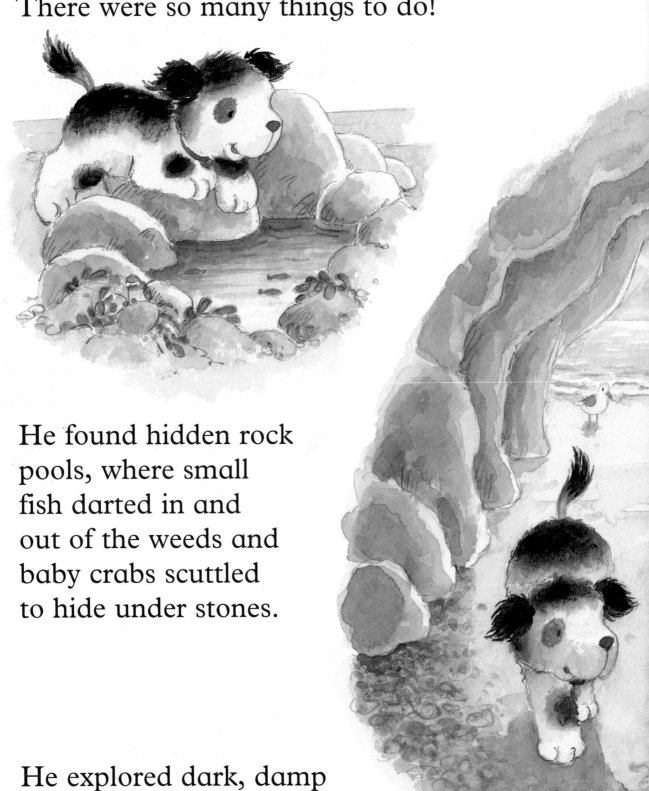

He found hidden rock
pools, where small
fish darted in and
out of the weeds and
baby crabs scuttled
to hide under stones.

He explored dark, damp
caves with strange, scary echoes.

He played games with Farmer Bob,
who threw sticks in the water
for him to fetch.

The next morning, Fergus woke early and went down to the beach on his own.
He was busy digging a hole in the sand when he noticed another dog watching him.

The dog looked friendly, so Fergus wagged his tail.

The dog
wagged his tail too, and
they both knew they could be friends.

Fergus had a new friend to play with!

Off they went, chasing each other across
the beach . . . "WOOF WOOF WOOF!"
and around the rocks . . .

"WOOF WOOF WOOF!"

Splashing through the waves . . .
"WOOF WOOF WOOF!"
and scaring the seagulls . . .
"WOOF WOOF WOOF!"

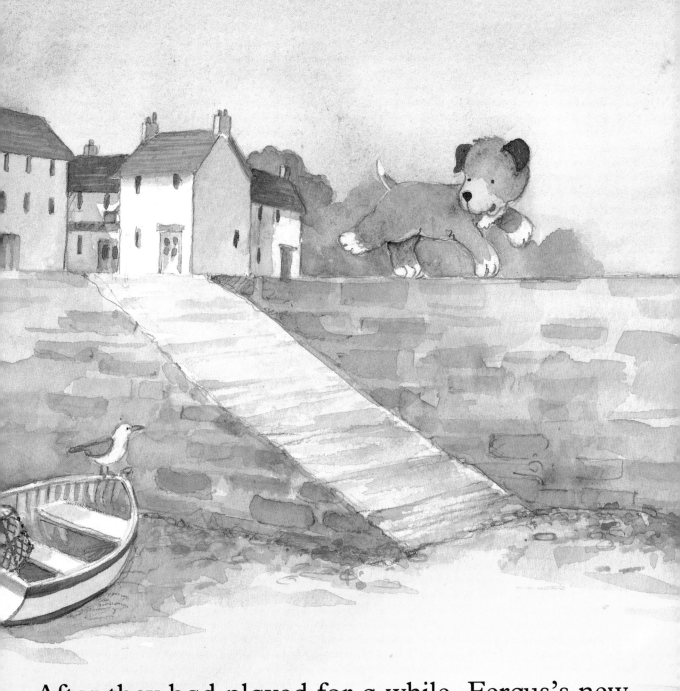

After they had played for a while, Fergus's new
friend ran up on to the long stone pier.
"WOOF WOOF!" he called over his shoulder.
He wanted Fergus to follow him . . .

A small fishing boat was
moored at the end of the pier.
The Captain was just about
to set sail.
"Come on, Salty!" he
called out. "We don't want
to miss the tide! Is your
friend coming too?"

This was going to be
an adventure!

Fergus and Salty lay on the deck as the Captain checked his crab pots. Sunlight sparkled on the lazy waves and seagulls swooped and swirled overhead.

"This is the life for me!" thought Fergus.

"So peaceful, and no farm animals to bother me. I should be a sea dog just like Salty!"

The Captain was pleased with his catch.
"There's a beauty!" he said proudly, holding
up one of the crabs. "Don't get too close . . .
unless you want your noses nipped!" he chuckled.

Suddenly Fergus's ears shot up.
He thought he'd heard a
strange noise coming
from the sea.

"Aaarf
Aaarf!"

There it was again! The same frightened cry.
"WOOF!" he said to Salty.
They crept to the side
of the boat to see what
was making the
noise, and
saw . . .

. . . a small baby seal!

The Captain came over to see.
"Looks like this little pup's in trouble!" he said.
"It probably swam out too far and is too tired to
swim back. Better take it back to its family."

Gently, he lifted the baby seal out of the water and on to the deck.

"Aaarf!" said the baby seal.
"WOOF!" said Fergus.

When the baby seal was safely back with its family, the Captain began putting on his sou'wester. "I can smell rain!" he said. "Better get home quick!"

Moments later, the sky darkened and raindrops began pattering on the wheelhouse roof where Fergus and Salty were sheltering.

Before long, the little fishing boat was being tossed up and down on giant waves, and heavy rain beat against the wheelhouse windows. Fergus huddled up to Salty as the Captain struggled to steer the boat. Everything seemed to be turning upside down and Fergus was beginning to feel very sick. "I wish I was back on the farm!" he groaned.

After what seemed like a very long time, they were safely back in the harbour. Fergus staggered up the steps on wobbly legs, then said goodbye to Salty and the Captain.

Cold and wet, he made his way
home to the holiday cottage.
He was pleased to see Farmer Bob
waiting at the garden gate.

Fergus snuggled into his comfy basket and closed his eyes. He thought about all the animals back at the farm. He couldn't wait to tell them of the things he'd done.

"Perhaps being a farm dog isn't so bad after all," he thought as he drifted off to sleep.